V.M. Fuentes

Table of Contents

Ankanowei

Essence of Nymph

Her laughter is the
echo of raindrops.

In sorrow tears of
shadow pour forth.

Joyous, she
radiates sunrise.

Breathes of wildflowers
flows from contentment.

Wrath of tempests, ever
raging against foes.

Her afterglow vanishes
decay for life.

In love, she sings
on the gentle breeze.

Fathomless depths
are her soul

The Seer

A robed figure ascended to
meet sleeping young man.

Blackened robes with burgundy
borders adorned It — eyes

of rich amethyst blazed beneath
the hood.

It glowered over as his body
shook and tossed
till It touched his forehead.

Awakened he grasped
scabbard with wooden beads

The figure snapped its skeletal
fingers and he stilled.

"Speak not yet heed
what must be known
and seen..."

Hazel eyes blinked in
fear mingled with amazement.

"It's coming, great change
perhaps for good...perhaps
not..."

The man pondered as the figure
sank beneath the floor to echo

"Harbinger are you, of change
and danger, beware for fate

is fluid..."

Soon the shadow cast
vanished as the floor

restored to normalcy
and man lay perplexed.

Returning to slumber, again
did heart constrict and body

shake as breath retreated
from mortal coil...

Opposites

They met on the horizon,
performing their duties

as their eyes drank in each
other's essence.

A glow seemed to emanate
from her fair skin.

Wheat-gold hair crowned
her and stormy eyes blazed.

Her lithe figure crossed to meet
him.

Shadow clung to his muscular
body.

Hazel eyes gazed steadfast
beneath raven hair.

Reaching each other, he began
to caress her face

warmth flooded his cold
fingers.

A quiver reverberated
and stilled their breathe.

A reaper, a forest nymph…
life and death.

Tempest

A blasphemy of storms
erases the desert of loneliness.

Lighting crystalizing sand in
a cloudy wake.

Columns of shadow traipse
across the battered field
pregnant with rain.

Drenching the earth in a torrent
of thunder,

wind deafening nature's voice
to beckon chaos.

The Willow Nymph

Never one to cease to smile against life's tumultuous winds,
casting spells of antiquity to withstand them crashing.

Woven in her liquid amber tresses are ever green flowers,
each dance to the gentle breeze wafting through...

Her lithe figure melds into Mother tree for peace and release,
wise to love at a time when it was scarce...such a rarity
for in a world of slashed wrists, pill popping, Janus faced others
her laugh carries a soothing balm yet to those who harm, a consequence of siren's call doth hasten their demise.

Her skin was as smooth birch expertly crafted to revel the soulful heartwood of Mother tree...

The forest paths were first worn by her footsteps, twas she
who discovered the mysteries of animal friends and the livelihood of trees and flowers.

Within her eyes lie strands of sapphire lightning and greying clouds, round iris bears a ring of gold.
The depths of which none have discovered...

Glimpses are seen of her figure, an afterglow if you will,
few happen upon her resting from travels near

Mother tree...

Parishad

The council convenes every
two hundred years, overseeing events
of land and kingdom.

First, a dragon monarch hailing from
the gale, ruling over sky, land, and sea,
imparting magik to siblings.

Second, faerie twins who conceive
flora across Ankanowei, imbuing
secrets to grass and shrub.

Third, siblings five, four, and three,
wield arcane crystals for magik
banned to inspire wisdom.

Lastly, Aesir king and queen
conquer stone and metal
building magnificence under mountains.

Humans disallowed, youngest of races,
impulsive and forgetful.

Revered above all for peace was
their making over six millennia.

Until magik became unbalanced
and blood was spilt.

Hephaestus, Thrown

Often, their father preferred a drunken
stupor to parenting,

where their mother hung smiles
around a bruised body.

They sat and played,
"hide and seek" forever
evading fist or dick.

It was a scroll that
cursed Braz, stealing
his leg.

Their father learned of Utrid's
fascination with reading
sounds,

and soon a jarl knocked,
soldiers arrested
more than Braz fathomed.

Three days.
Three days of freedom bought
their family suffering

for their last gift was
Braz's promise to
a corpse

several paces away
from a new leg,
broken and twisted.

Altepetl

Woven through streets cerulean waves
caressed hallowed stone and shell.

Pearls littered houses poor and rich
while splintered calci flourished
along stairs

leading guest and citizen to
chilling depths.

Beauty enraptured serpent scales
who taught Petrichor children
secrets of ocean and creek.

Boats were naught but human
contraptions for Petrichor enchanters
wove water itself.

Sunkissed skin was their pride
and sea salt their perfume.

Ever friend to Nereids and sea creature
alike Petrichor citizens traded
secrets to water Ankanowei.

Yet, peace reigned on the horizon
and beneath the stars, lacking
the foresight to see betrayal

in Light and Blood.

The Silent One

The lasting survivor of history's blemish,
his concubine throttled
the remaining warlocks
with blood magik.

The debasement of virtue was
their soul and temptation
their creed.

Using bone and tendon,
ring and gem,
enacting a curse
stealing immortality.

A stew of veritable warning
sent them gulping down
a concoction of woe.

He forced himself still as the
curse took hold.

Draining skin pale,
painting magik crimson,
sharpening tooth to fang.

She rose first, leaving him
writhing to test her renewal.

Ire of Hades

Scintillating flames sever flesh
atop jaundiced bone.

Hampering shrieks squeeze
through earthquakes
as crushed
throats freeze.

Sitting among dank caverns
and green fire is a
winnowing
king.

Sole keeper of bejeweled
magik among his
followers

and secrets to death
itself.

He waits,
scheming, engaged in a
fated game,

leaving nothing to
chance.

Relief sweeps across the surface,
sea, and sky, hoping his
return is forgone,
yet, he waits

for bones and fangs to be free.

Stained

Crumbling pictures petrified in
normalcy
as if it never happened.

Structures suspended by sour
rainbows, they warn animals
and travelers of
ancestral mistakes.

Corpses, long faded to rot,
poison stone and root.

Shattered crystals embedded in
walls and trees,
twinkle beneath sun
and moon.

Magik is absent in the air,
enveloped by silence.

Irthqua

Born of flesh and marrow
they are the beast tamers,
teaching fowl and ant
how to live.

Gifting the first creatures
with speech before
binding souls.

Now, skin is never seen
only fur, scale, or feather
and two are
one.

The first creatures lived
in peace but not all
were soulbound.

Yet, the Irthqua gave
them protection,
respecting choice
and balance.

Over land, air, and sea
they roamed wielding
a magik envied
by Light.

They kept the scales
despite jealousy
and oversaw the
migration of
dragons.

Wood for crystal

Magik is for the immortals, the gods, creators of
Ankanowei to weave and sing.

Yet, here on the lands, beneath the ocean, and dark
caverns the children of the Five
were held in contempt.

Jealous and fearful of their power,
bound they were to crystals
for wood was their
life.

By siblings two and three,
for nothing could
bind them.

Equality was necessary for balance
even the creators deemed it so.

The children consented, never
considering how lovely
crystals were nor
the wisdom
that lay in
their
colors.

Crystal Spires

Seared by moonlight, desert sand
sprouted, erecting buildings
of purest glass.

The ArchMage and his sons spent
weeks imbuing glass with protection spells,

his daughters crowned the
spires in stars to watch
above.

None in the desert could match
its splendor.

An oasis of liquid glass among
torrid air that Magi
call, "Home."

Eclipses capture its rainbow
essence and shimmering
music.

On the verge of greatness
till jealousy settled
in the pages
of a book.

Humans

Impulsive, grown, created on a whim
to balance the other races
or
a cruel joke.

Still, they fester like a plague,
dying sooner than flowers
but tinkering like dwarves.

Naïve to the stories of Ankanowei,
ignorant to magik's role,
a lifeline.

They frolic and war over petty
matters, leaving pity or disdain
for their magical betters.

Its only a guess how long they'll
survive between magik
and ruin.

Yet, they resist like the faithful
ants working till they drop
for a minute of peace.

Mishipeshu

Spotted fur drowned crocodiles
in rivers before
escaping to oceans.

A coppery sheen lingers
where blood disappears.

Beneath the surface, antlers
ripple waves to pierce
stones.

Its waterlogged purr entices
the unknown beast,
curious.

Those of wisdom and caution
left its shores for greener
plains.

Such a change from when the
Lynx first growled and
water flourished

before the death of its wife…

Cursed Skin

Two souls intwined to sacrifice
for power untenable,
rage.

Insanity shreds their transformation,
howling in light and darkness
it roams.

Begone blood and forsake
sanctuary to rival
ruin.

Its eyes,
The eyes conceal the curse
and its tongue reveal it.

Friend and foe alike are
felled by them.

Few ever chose the exiled
path for the power
only lasts in
rage.

Pinnacle of Learning

Scrolls fumble in jealousy of
its younger brother — books

The Magi, in their haste, forgot
to contain the magiks bound
in scrolls to preserve their
legacy.

Instead, it leaks out
mimicking their authors'
temperament.

Only Mages are permitted
inside the grand library
for this reason.

For all the old knowledge
is gathered there, while

public libraries hold barely
current histories and spells.

It was there that writing
took its form from air to page
documenting language and time.

The Craft

Creativity

Imagination isn't all skyrockets and naked beasts,
but the single spark to a wildfire that
paints the world in nonexistent color

It breaks time and transcends death
for nothing can restrain its
form

Harken to secrets of masks
and shadow, where
vocation sears minds

Taxing, freeing, unmitigated
pursuit of expression

if only to realize inspiration
was there all the while

Writing

Its Mozart or Beethoven
single draft or several,
else the mind wanders

Wherein word or page,
concealing subconscious
revelation to readers

Yet, buried in psyche lies
scribbles and death,
erasers and life

Worlds from beyond the
veil, shared humanity,
span centuries

Voices collect dust
from drawing sounds

as the muse speaks
or demons tarry

Bellowing past frenzied
to fantasy
and reality

giving immortality
to those of us
who glimpse
beyond the veil

The Work

Days passed, weeks, months, when the pen stops.
The unhinged mind forgets alignment, enabling
a Sisyphean struggle to write one word
any word will do.

Other times, words flow as ink bleeds into paper
while the mind ceases to think, rather it
halts.

Surprising? Hopefully not.

Each artistic flourish and pained sentence
bears a writer's soul, for
words are always a reflection.

Whether blatant or not, remember as
selection takes place and disdain
creeps along the wrist,

it is here where dragons fly,
space holds more universes,
monsters have tea,
cannibals delight in vegan,
and
the sea fits into a vast thimble
those dreams become
reality

and fiction is nothing more than a
love letter to the world.

Yet, how else can a writer communicate
their perceptions, illustrating society's horrors

and humankind's errors
while evolving the struggle to
hope?

Continue till the work is done. Finished.
Even death cannot cease these worlds
for they survive in infamy, profanity,
and happily remind you
that you are not alone.

Editing

"Frankenstein" ring any bells?
or
are you partial to necromancy?

The words stripped ~~away~~ to ~~the~~ marrow,
~~with?~~ only tendon ~~to~~ stitches them
in place.

Course ~~the~~ organs are mismatched
and try not to worry about the veins
everywhere ~~everything does go to goes where~~
~~its supposed to,~~

~~to~~ they carry ~~the plot~~ characters
wherever they're needed,
be it tragedy or
~~unsuspecting~~ gratitude.

A masochistic method of
agony and relief ~~to~~
~~produce~~ a finished
piece.

Everlasting

Love is what poets dream of,
Giving life to souls, happiness in daydreams
Where sorrow is pleasurable and fate—jealous.

But tarry here, death and despair ferret out
hopes to circumvent joy, a languishing
attempt at hostility.

Cultural Identity

Hidden beneath squalor of mind
is shame for one's heritage.

Grown fondness for a classical
education, I resigned learning
patched history,

in favor of steady curriculum
and American values.

Heavy handedness influenced
my quill till it reeked of
shame.

Struggling to find identity
until I admitted my
reticence
and sought the
burial of my ancestors

to revive the soul and
imbue my quill
with blood.

Publish or Perish!

The hideous reality of pressure from nonsensical
public, academic, and private
inadequacy for writers.

> Here we struggle under
> lamplight and drizzling
> anxiety from the voices
> rattling eardrums.

Still, the tap tap tap, clickity clack
nothing new to writers old
and young.

> We're here plowing away
> as time steals inky
> sweat.

Debtor to the muse, the talent
calls us home to create
the art we were
always meant
to.

"Less is more-"

A winnowing truth that cauterizes classic literature

and any attempts to emulate them

Epics are rarer than water and grammar berates the

fledgling into conformity

Conciseness is key, yet some sentences must be

extensive while lacking commas and irreparable

periods

Writer's block

That lasted longer than I thought…how do you get over this?

No one knows but everyone has their own recipe.

Anything from Hemmingway's tonic to staring at a wall wondering where you're going from here and why life is shit.

Or take a walk. Get off the phone. Turn on the tube. Do something or nothing.

If it works it works, just don't-

Listen

The legacy of those forgotten in the pages of time
are nowhere but the memories of
the dead.
        Sometimes the soul stirs
         triggered by universal
          song, "Come and see."
Begone drivel,
experience wonder and
happenstance,
life is ever so easy.
        Homeward bound,
         the heart flutters
          hoping to
          be heard.

The Journey

Before religion, I knew,
ink over blood.

Between magik and gods,
pen wove a fabric of
changing dreams.

I didn't realize how far I'd
come before publishing.

Took years to achieve a
glimpse of Ankanowei.

Buried in libraries of
authors past, my
soul returned.

In between assignments
and tragedy, my hands
created dreams.

An ink-stained path till
fate is revealed…

My life

It's solitary work like death, in the end
writing is best done alone.

A muse or a half-crazed demon
invokes madness in the
bones

sending pens into fury,
cracking keyboards,
sending the shrill of
typewriters to
oblivion.

Dreams of worlds within
worlds come to life
and die from edits.

Yet, the memories live on
in soulful murmurs
and thoughts.

A Natural?

"It's a skill, like anything else
in life it takes time."

Few born with a silver tongue
or a ready quill.

Rather, the craft is honed with
every stroke made in
haste or hurry

for a perfect moment
is scarce.

Writer vs Author

Distinguishable by publishing
success, nothing more.

Neither are more proficient
than the other.

Some achieve the fame and
sales but both cannot
turn away from
the pen.

I have been both on
occasion, yet
"Writer" is
my preference.

It's not just a title
or status but
a vocation,

part of the artistry
in life.

Feel no disregard for
either if you are
worried,

instead remember
both are valued.

A Smattering of Poetry

The Empty

The roundabout room where sitting was natural
and memories traipse across the rug.

Tickling shoes in the midnight glare
of starlight.

A chilling gale wafts from barren
fireplace, reminding guests of
your absence.

Pictures haunt every nook and corner,
carrying your pleasant smile.

Sniffling laughter and bickering ensue,
cause family should seldom avoid
disagreement.

Lingering in your room, they finally
left in group or single file.

One turned, hand on light switch,
catching the flickering bulb,
a lasting gaze before
closing your
door.

Burning on the Battlefield

As I lay upon a mound of
dirt, breathing in dry
air, weariness overcome
me as the stench of
burning flesh invaded my
nostrils.

All but deaf from
the cacophony of gun fire
around me, naught but
incessant ringing did
plague me as I lay.

My head rolled to the side
to gaze upon the tattered
remnants of my friend, my companion, my lover...

His face once chiseled by
angels now shredded
by shrapnel.

Half his torso
engulfed in ravenous flame.

Voiceless I shriek till my
throat went raw and
eyes stung from filthy
tears,

crawling with but one arm
and eviscerated legs
towards my beloved...

that death might

extend but a single mercy
to die by my beloved
upon the burning
battlefield.

Ageless

The tree grows strong
with roots entrenched.

Leafy branches hold sway
over the wind as they bend.

The tiny pink blossoms
mature...then float away.

Do you love?

A flower's first bloom should be cherished,
if not for its beauty than for its rarity.

The wind may howl, rain plunder and feet trample
yet, it stands...

Let it bloom unhindered and without selfishness,
why should it bloom only for you?

Its lavish stem, vermillion spots,
and onyx petals, reflect its splendor
among the dreary world.

As the breeze ferries its
song away, remember its fragrance.

Remember how marvelous it bloomed
beneath sapphire skies.

Alone

The pestilence of life is something untenable

or risky.

A lasting effect of human nature to

conceive the imperceptible.

Still, among gleeful smiles and

loving arms, apathy swarms

in.

Tingling the bittersweet notion of

family.

Beneath a crisp blue sun,

I languish in the squalor

of heartbeats.

Caring

As the tree grows
beneath obsidian soil,
water pours from the
dented bucket.

Rays enrich its crusted
bark and veiny leaves
whilst he prunes
cracked branches.

Before the moon retreats
he lays against
the hardened trunk
as stars shimmer.

It becomes difficult to

be water and rain, stirring
swirling, and bubbling
even the downpour isn't as
common
as it could be or should be.

Not a cloud goes by do
I mention a ride,
"Pick me, I'll come!"

Yet, they move past
Unhindered by winds or sun,
only stopping for thunder
and lightning.

But here I stay, filthy from
oil and mud that
goes
with cans, bottles, and
trash, perhaps a
gun or two
even a body once a
week.

No, it's not as
difficult as it could be,
but why change now?

A good morning

The last rung coiled round my neck as Jormungandr began its thundering blunder known as the Last of Days. Or Ragnarok to you learned folk. But to me, it was little more than a nuisance. For while the whole of Midgard stood to panic and war against foes of yore; I turned to bade all, "Shut It! There's sleep to be had!"

Of the thundering sky shouted the irresponsible Tor, riding his minuscule chariot, beckoning warriors of new birth and old death, "Come! War is here! Dust off those beards of blood. Sharpen those rusty swords and shields. Let not your axes be dull for War is here!"

Yet, fair Loki plays his tricks and picks at the Lyre of Sorrow only to find that which is gone forevermore. Consumed be earthen heavens and chilling seas as Night rules while Loki dies.

Only to that, I say, "Play it in B Minor. Death is hardly more cheerful in Major C."
As fathers cry for their sons and mothers their daughters meeting the dip of inferno to shadow. Where all is lost to golden isles hidden beneath twilit skies.

And there shall it begin, "Sleep at last."

Mismatched Socks

Must we always find joy in our own thoughts, those
being fair are hardly ones recognizing until the
moment passes.

Or are they, truly and really fair? Of blackened
shadow do some persist and relish those perishable,
fully bent on eradicating those adversaries.

While others dutifully, either by pleasure or tradition,
are comforted by memories fair.

Naught for ill are thought and action conceived, yet
are they consistent in sprouting along books,
television, and phones.

If one can see with eyes their own reflection spies
back in laughter, for none are always wholly good.

Beneath glasses parting

were rows of loving tapes and records.
Lovers and haters alike roamed those
plastic tapes and vinyl circles.

Denied pleasant or wanting ears
stirred with unholy slumber as they

lay covered in a decade's dusting
or two. Left under ivory walls and

decrepit halls of past fathers and sons,
where mothers and daughters are
scantly browsed.

Only to die of wanting, of yearning
for the delight of immortality.

But as the years pass on
shelved the discarded

are they begging for another
turn...

We aren't what we could be...

Through summer's mourn and
winter's bloom humans thrive
to survive...and thus created
automatons, siege engines,
and machinations to prove
glory beyond reckoning.

Yet, beneath these innovations
lie bloody sinew, splintered bone
and echoes of child shrieks...

Again, thrust into violence
amidst achievements in the psyche,
biology, and physics are what
humans can't help.

Crimson orchids
sprout beneath the
skeletal remains of ancestors
and watered by tears of
descendants.

If only

the moment was like any other,
average.

No Hollywood highlights or
pomp and circumstance
just a "Hello."

Maybe then the agony, born of
loss, would dissipate.

"I'm sorry," can cease to be
meaningful since overuse
remains pitiful.

Desolate

Over the years, I've spent days
counting minutes of loneliness
as romance fails.

Ever the watcher, a third wheel of
sorts, giver of advice and support
rather than--honeycombs

chills in summer and icicles in
winter, yes more clichés.

An endless void where my tears
have fled, drying a withering
soul to leather.

Steps and breaths are all it takes
to beckon a forgotten yearning.

Yet, the mirror speaks truth
as decay breeds loneliness in
my crow's feet.

Greying hairs invade my curls
before I can remember
how to smile again.

Left Behind

The waves licked at my feet
Listening to the voice
Of one who should have
Died.

I loved you before rain knew its path
And thunder was a shout.

Rather to survive the memory
Of you lay entombed in earth and
Stone.

I loved you before earth grew in seeds
And flowers were petals.

Still, I see your face in clouds
And shadows of my eyes
A glimpse of your afterglow.

I loved you before moon birthed stars
And sun was a campfire.

I scattered the ashes, no more silence
As the waves lapped you up.
Traveling where?

Only you know,
For this journey is forlorn
And not for lovers…

Barrage

I can't stop these feckless
attempts to control the
ferocity of my mind.

The thoughts change through
the gates of my consciousness
be it eye, ear, nose, or mouth

even touch betrays me here.

Nothing impedes my propensity
to worry and fear for inevitable
failures that may not pass, each
unlikely as the next.

But nothing terrifies me more than
discover, how will I escape then?

Will I be abandoned? Left
to my own devices, exiled
from family and friends

with only my shadow
to accompany me?

Same as the rest I guess
none can understand me
more than others but I'll never
know

cause I haven't spoken
to another person in
five years.

Fading Glory

The afterglow of Euripides
was less tempting than a
honeycomb buried in hornets

across the way, I saw the
lonely vulture scouring
towards extinction

above the birdsong, I hear
city lights hum and
tires screeching, racing away

maps erase green with grey
appearing less diverting
each year

oh, the smells changed the most,
flowers are less crisp to
touch, shedding forgotten fragrance

treasure the oasis of dreams
hidden by a green haze
and shallow loves.

"I'm sorry"

Disagreements turn to frustration
and haphazard thoughts
ruminating over the
less than goodness of the
heart

or so we're told.

A slight is misconceived
and done away with in
a hurry.

The weakness of this is the
forgoing of, "I'm sorry."

Such a frivolous phrase, mocked
as cliché but how else
can we say it?

Yes, changing action is
warranted but without words
how will action be given
significance?

About the Author

V.M. Fuentes recently published, "Simmering Lifetimes." The first anthology containing every poetry book V.M. Fuentes has self-published: Bittersweet Things, A Corpse Parade, We're Still Here, and A Greying Horizon. In his early twenties, he acquired a BA in Creative Writing and an MA in Forensic Psychology to enhance his creative prowess and understanding of human nature. While getting his doctorate, V.M. Fuentes is working on self-publishing his first fantasy novel filled with arcane spells and fantastical creatures. When not delving into his magical world, V.M. Fuentes enjoys reading, drinking too much tea, and spending an absurd amount of time on his laptop.

Twitter: @VFue5
Instagram: vm_fuentes
Website: www.vmfuentes.com

www.ingramcontent.com/pod-product-compliance
Lightning Source LLC
Chambersburg PA
CBHW060913130726
48001CB00006B/2219